Gates of Gold

by Frank McGuinness

CHICAGO PUBLIC LIBRARY

REFERENCE

Form 178 rev. 01-07

A SAMUEL FRENCH ACTING EDITION

SAMUEL FRENCH

FOUNDED 1830

NEW YORK HOLLYWOOD LONDON TORONTO

SAMUELFRENCH.COM

ISBN 978-0-573-69735-7   Printed in U.S.A.   #29178

MUSIC USE NOTE

Licensees are solely responsible for obtaining formal written permission from copyright owners to use copyrighted music in the performance of this play and are strongly cautioned to do so. If no such permission is obtained by the licensee, then the licensee must use only original music that the licensee owns and controls. Licensees are solely responsible and liable for all music clearances and shall indemnify the copyright owners of the play and their licensing agent, Samuel French, Inc., against any costs, expenses, losses and liabilities arising from the use of music by licensees.

IMPORTANT BILLING AND CREDIT
REQUIREMENTS

All producers of *GATES OF GOLD must* give credit to the Author of the Play in all programs distributed in connection with performances of the Play, and in all instances in which the title of the Play appears for the purposes of advertising, publicizing or otherwise exploiting the Play and/or a production. The name of the Author *must* appear on a separate line on which no other name appears, immediately following the title and *must* appear in size of type not less than fifty percent of the size of the title type.

GATES OF GOLD was produced by Warren Baker and Sally Jacobs, The Artists' Theatre Group at Theater B on February 19, 2009 in New York City. The performance was directed by Kent Paul, with sets by Michael Schweikardt, costumes by Nanzi Adzima, lighting by Phil Monat, hair design by Leone Gagliardi, original music by Robert C. Rees, casting by Barry Moss. The production technical director was Jason Adams, production electrician was Amy Harper, and the production properties master was Sven Nelson. The production stage manager was Kathleen E.G. Munroe. The cast was as follows:

KASSIE	Diane Ciesla
ALMA	Kathleen McNenny
RYAN	Seth Numrich
GABRIEL	Martin Rayner
CONRAD	Charles Shaw Robinson

CHARACTERS

(In order of appearance)

GABRIEL – 60s
CONRAD – 60s
KASSANDRA – 50s, 60s
ALMA – 20s, 30s
RYAN – 20s

Scene One

*(In the bedroom **GABRIEL**, expertly, barely applies make-up before the mirror. In the living room **CONRAD** stands behind the armchair. **ALMA** sits on the couch.)*

CONRAD. I think it is fair to warn you, Gabriel will not be the easiest of patients.

ALMA. Jesus, does he speak Swedish?

CONRAD. Swedish?

ALMA. The last one I nursed, she spoke Swedish – morning, noon and night. Nearly drove me demented. But in the end I picked up a few words. We got into conversation. And she left me a dictionary in her will.

CONRAD. A Swedish dictionary?

ALMA. English.

CONRAD. Why?

ALMA. She caught on I was never a great speller. So I looked on the bright side.

CONRAD. Do you still possess it?

ALMA. Don't use the word possess. It smacks to me of the devil.

CONRAD. Do you believe in the devil?

ALMA. I believe in nothing. I've watched people dying. I've heard them breathing their last. Gasping. There's no devil. There's no God. There's just people panicking.

CONRAD. You're not afraid of death?

ALMA. I'm not afraid of life. I'm a bit afraid of children. Sometimes they tell the truth.

CONRAD. Gabriel does resemble a child at times.

ALMA. No, he doesn't. He's an old man.

CONRAD. He's younger than I am.

ALMA. So am I. What's your problem?

CONRAD. Miss –

ALMA. Campbell. Alma Campbell. That's my name, Alma.

CONRAD. Miss Campbell –

ALMA. You don't like me. I don't care if you do. The man in that bedroom is dying from a shortage of breath. I know about that way of dying. Are you giving me a job?

GABRIEL. Hire her.

CONRAD. You've a sharp tongue, Miss Campbell, and I don't think you are aware of who it is you're nursing.

GABRIEL. A dying old fool who's getting his comeuppance.

CONRAD. This is a man who has distinguished the theatrical profession for more than forty years.

GABRIEL. The bitch, I am only thirty-three. Admittedly that was in a previous existence. I don't like to talk about it.

CONRAD. He has served the stage as an actor, a writer, a designer and a director.

GABRIEL. He did not excel in all of these –

CONRAD. He did not excel in any of these –

GABRIEL. I have heard your words and will keep them in my heart.

CONRAD. Still, these onerous duties have taken their toll on him. He can no longer touch alcohol –

GABRIEL. Oh, boo-hoo.

CONRAD. He's always been devoutly religious. He's growing even more so.

GABRIEL. Listen to Our Lady of Fatima.

CONRAD. I don't believe you're right for this job. I too have a sharp tongue. You have failed this audition.

ALMA. Audition?

CONRAD. Young woman, I'm a busy man – I have no time –

ALMA. – to nurse a difficult bastard that's blown every nurse you've hired so hard out of the water that her arse left the imprint of itself on the front door. I'm willing to give it a go, are you?

CONRAD. Why?

ALMA. You are desperate.

CONRAD. Is he dying?

ALMA. Yes.

GABRIEL. No.

> (silence)

No.

CONRAD. Is he aware of that?

GABRIEL. Yes.

ALMA. No.

CONRAD. Can you, as the Irish say, put manners on him?

ALMA. Manners?

CONRAD. Can you prepare him for dying?

> (silence)

I warn you, Gabriel does not like the truth.

ALMA. Neither do I.

CONRAD. I didn't think you did.

ALMA. Then I have the job?

CONRAD. Are you that desperate?

ALMA. Do I have the job?

> (CONRAD *sits in the armchair and looks at* ALMA.
> GABRIEL *tries to stand and nearly falls. He steadies
> himself against the table. A strange light intensifies on
> the joint portrait. He is breathing with difficulty. He
> makes his way to the bed and sits there.*)

GABRIEL. Our eyes met.

> (a sharp breath)

Not our eyes, our faces touched.

> (a sharp breath)

Do you remember my face when I was young? And you
were always older, an old man. Always sensible – always
accurate. Always.

> (a sharp breath)

ALMA. There's not much work for nurses at the minute.

GABRIEL. There's not much work for actors at the minute.

ALMA. I'm willing to clean your man's arse, but I'm not going to lick yours.

GABRIEL. I think we should do something brave.

ALMA. What did you mean by audition?

GABRIEL. We should start a theatre and do the work we want to do.

ALMA. I'll need living quarters here if I'm to nurse him properly.

(a series of sharp breaths)

I know next to nothing about you. I know you're queers – I couldn't give a tinker's curse. I've been warned and I don't care. I need a job. You said it, I'm desperate.

GABRIEL. I swear I'll be good, I'll behave.

ALMA. What's your answer?

GABRIEL. I'm not asking you to love me. I'm asking you to live with me.

CONRAD. You're not up to him.

ALMA. I'm willing to make an effort.

GABRIEL. Can we try?

CONRAD. It won't last.

ALMA. Have you had any better offer?

CONRAD. It can't last.

GABRIEL. Who else would love you? I know how you hate yourself. I know how you hide what you are from yourself. I've heard you at night.

(a sharp breath)

Weeping –

(a sharp breath)

Weeping –

(a sharp breath)

Weeping.

CONRAD. He believes himself still to be a beautiful man.

GABRIEL. So frightened they would laugh at you – Women.

CONRAD. Can you respect that lie he persists in telling to himself?

GABRIEL. I won't let them laugh – I won't laugh –

CONRAD. He is not a fool, but he is a liar.

GABRIEL. Love me.

ALMA. I've nursed old men. I've nursed old women. I've nursed children. I've nursed the dying.

CONRAD. Gasping for breath.

ALMA. Gasping.

GABRIEL. Hire her.

CONRAD. You're hired.

ALMA. So are you.

Scene Two

(Dawn is breaking. The sitting room is in darkness. A light burns softly in the bedroom. GABRIEL lies awake in bed. ALMA, near sleep, sits singing lowly to keep herself awake. She hums, 'I dreamt I dwelt in marble halls', occasionally singing some words.)

GABRIEL. My mother sang that when I was a child, in Spain.

ALMA. I didn't know you were Spanish?

GABRIEL. I was born in Salamanca. My mother was of Irish descent – a descendant of the Wild Geese, the Irish aristocrats who fled to Europe. My father was a priest – a student priest at the Irish seminary of Salamanca. They could not be married but she reared me. Each year on her birthday, May the twenty-second, a yellow rose would be left on her doorstep. That was her name, Rosa – for St. Rose of Lima, a Peruvian anchorite willingly buried alive in the walls of a convent, burning with love of God. My mother turned into an anchorite burning with love for my father. She never left the walls of our house after I was born in Salamanca. And I never, ever saw my father. Sing more – sing me another song.

(She sings a verse from 'Cutting the corn down in Cresshlough today'.)

ALMA. Dear Danny, I'm taking the pen in my hand
To tell you we're just out of sight of the land.
In a big anchor liner we're sailing away
And we're leaving old Ireland for ever today.
Oh It's good to be you who is taking your tay
Where they're cutting the corn down in Cresshlough today.

GABRIEL. You have a good voice, but a man should sing that song. I can remember my father used to, when I was a child, on our ranch in the Argentine. He emigrated from Ireland to work as a cowboy and he struck lucky. He met my mother –

ALMA. St. Rose of Lima –

GABRIEL. That was her name, yes. Lima. She was born there.

ALMA. In Peru?

GABRIEL. Peru. Now she was performing with a circus troupe in Buenos Aires. The woman was a natural on the flying trapeze. The night he attended, didn't she fall? He raced into the circus ring and caught her in his arms. Extraordinary I know, but the truly extraordinary thing was, this Peruvian girl spoke fluent Connemara Gaelic. She'd learned it from a sailor who'd been a student priest in the Irish seminary –

ALMA. In Salamanca.

GABRIEL. You have remarkable powers of deduction. My father married her, but the tragedy was he didn't speak a word of Gaelic as he was from Wales. Argentina is overrun with Welsh people! They are all called Jones and they do unspeakable things with wooden spoons.

ALMA. How many fathers and mothers do you have?

GABRIEL. As many as are necessary to survive them. They tend to die but not to fade away. So it's imperative to remember every detail about them, particularly those details they could never have known themselves. That way they might still live, or is that the medication speaking?

ALMA. You tell me – that's what I'm here for.

GABRIEL. To listen to me babble?

ALMA. You speak lovely. My old fella rarely spoke. The mother wouldn't let him get a word in. A bit of a mismatch. I put it down to geography. He was from Kerry. She was a Dublin woman, through and through. The woman never shut her mouth. Such a load of *rameis* –

GABRIEL. *Rameis?*

ALMA. Kerry word. Means nonsense. I only heard my da crack one joke in his life. He told Ma *rameis* means wisdom. He'd say, 'Woman, you are full of *rameis*.' She would beam scarlet with pleasure. I suppose she must

ALMA. *(cont.)* have loved him. He was a handsome fellow
when he was younger. Image of my brother. My
brother was the image of my father.

GABRIEL. Was?

ALMA. Car accident. God. My twin. Gone. You should be
sleeping. I'm keeping you awake. You'll have to shut
me up. I learned the gift of the gab from Ma.

GABRIEL. Did he look like you?

ALMA. My father?

GABRIEL. Your twin brother?

ALMA. You'd know we were brother and sister.

GABRIEL. I have a sister. She has a son.

ALMA. I know. They're coming to visit you. Are you up to
seeing them?

GABRIEL. Her – yes. Him – him –

ALMA. Your nephew?

GABRIEL. He has broken my heart.

ALMA. My brother broke many a heart. Eejit. I can get word
to put them off.

GABRIEL. No, this is their house. It will be. His house.
Conrad will see to that.

ALMA. Lucky to have it all arranged so there's no fights.

GABRIEL. No fights, yes.

ALMA. Do you get on with your sister?

GABRIEL. She too has the gift of gab. Did you get on with
your brother?

ALMA. I'll pass on that. Listen, you've to tell me when you
need anything. I'll do what I can. I don't believe in suffering for the sake of it.

GABRIEL. I do.

ALMA. Then that's the difference between us.

GABRIEL. Perhaps. Who knows?

ALMA. Jesus, now you are sounding like my father. Who
knows? His old refrain. Da, can we have bicycles for
Christmas? Who knows? Can we have roller skates?
Who knows?

GABRIEL. *Qui sait?* Guy de Maupassant wrote a short story called 'Qui Sait?' Who knows? I barely remember what it was about. Something to do with suffering. What was the point of suffering?

ALMA. Fuck all, sunshine. That French boy would know that if he'd seen what I have.

GABRIEL. You must tell me all you've seen, my dear.

ALMA. Call me by my name – it's Alma.

GABRIEL. How terribly Latinate.

(**CONRAD** *appears in the living room where light has broken through. He has been asleep in the armchair all night.*)

Alma – beloved. Alma mater – beloved mother.

ALMA. Don't call me that. I'm nobody's mother. I never will be.

(silence)

GABRIEL. I do apologise.

ALMA. I can be extremely touchy. I may be just your nurse –

GABRIEL. Why aren't you a doctor?

(silence)

ALMA. That was for boys.

GABRIEL. Your brother –

ALMA. Had no interest.

GABRIEL. He was beautiful?

ALMA. Very.

GABRIEL. You were in the car with him?

ALMA. Yes.

GABRIEL. You weren't hurt?

ALMA. Not a hair on my head. He was driving. And he was drunk. Fuck him. Let that be an end. Why did I open my mouth?

GABRIEL. You're your mother's daughter.

ALMA. You have an answer for everything.

GABRIEL. Perhaps.

ALMA. Who knows? I've been lying all the time, by the way.

GABRIEL. Somehow I don't believe that.

ALMA. Somehow I don't believe you do.

GABRIEL. You see, I think you tell the truth. How near is death?

ALMA. Near enough.

GABRIEL. Will it be quick?

ALMA. Are you frightened of that?

GABRIEL. Will it be dirty?

ALMA. It always is.

GABRIEL. I'd dislike that. I'd be frightened of that. In that dreadful hospital doing those endless tests they made me drink this revolting stuff to make me shit and shit and shit until I smelt of nothing but what I was drinking – then I was frightened, for I was a fucking, filthy old man, dying in his own dirt. The only consolation is, I'm now ready to play King Lear. His problem is not dementia. It's diarrhoea.

ALMA. Remind me not to miss it. I was never a great one for going to plays. For me it's a waste of time and money. I just sleep through the whole show. Then I wake up at the end and I'm pissed angry with myself.

GABRIEL. Because you missed the performance?

ALMA. Because I missed the interval.

(CONRAD *enters the bedroom. It is now daylight.*)

CONRAD. Alma, go and have some rest, please. I've slept well. We'll manage for a while on our own.

GABRIEL. Conrad has always managed to sleep. It's such an endearing characteristic. I do think his capacity to snatch forty winks defines him. That's why I refer to him affectionately as my log. 'Good morning, my log. So glad to see you, my log. You look refreshed and well, my log.'

(*silence*)

GABRIEL. *(cont.)* And how are you, Gabriel? Well, Mother here is still alive and kicking. This is a wonder considering the poor old chorus girl has spent the night in a delirium of drugs and obscene dreams.

CONRAD. Then I hope you enjoyed them.

GABRIEL. It is dreadful – dreadful to be dying.

CONRAD. I wouldn't know.

GABRIEL. You will. And It delights me to inform you that dying is remarkably like being stuck in a traffic jam through Limerick.

CONRAD. I have never been through Limerick. If I have, I've sensibly suppressed the memory.

GABRIEL. May God and Limerick forgive you.

CONRAD. I'll take my chance with God. Limerick I leave to your devices.

GABRIEL. Has there ever been any man I have hated more than you?

CONRAD. Your wigmaker?

GABRIEL. I divorce you – I divorce you – I divorce you. We are separated in the eyes of Allah.

CONRAD. Muslims stone men like us, my love.

GABRIEL. I would welcome a little light stoning. It might ease my agony.

CONRAD. Are you truly in agony?

GABRIEL. Yes.

CONRAD. Good.

ALMA. Jesus, I'm off to my bed. You two must have been some tulips in your prime.

GABRIEL. Tulips? Prime? How dare you –

(He has a breathing fit. CONRAD panics.)

CONRAD. Gabriel – Alma – Gabriel –

(The breathing fit stops.)

GABRIEL. I'm doing my wounded hostess. The kiss of life is not necessary. Where was I? Prime – tulips – this woman compares me to that flatulent Dutch flower?

GABRIEL. *(cont.)* I am *la dame aux camélias*, I am a lily of the valley, I am a rose of Lima, and I bear no resemblance to a tulip. She has crossed me, Conrad. Fire her – fire her on the spot.

CONRAD. You're fired.

ALMA. Right you be.

GABRIEL. This day I disown you, though you may be my only daughter. I send you from this house into sleet and snow.

ALMA. Grand, I love the winter.

GABRIEL. It breaks my heart that you have been so – so –

ALMA. Ungrateful?

GABRIEL. Ungrateful. Goodbye. You may not kiss me.

ALMA. Jesus, you're a right pantomime. Wake me when I need you. I mean when you need me. Give me a couple of hours.

GABRIEL. Alma?

(silence)

Don't drink and drive.

ALMA. You may not kiss me.

(She leaves.)

CONRAD. You like her, don't you?

GABRIEL. I liked a lot of girls. Especially the ones I could exchange frocks with. Alma does not remind me of them. Her dress sense is entirely Canadian.

CONRAD. She's worked out much better than I thought.

GABRIEL. I hate your schoolmarm persona.

CONRAD. You seem to have good fun with her.

GABRIEL. She's quite devoted to you.

CONRAD. Me? No, you –

GABRIEL. I am not well. Not well at all. That's what you say, Gabriel is not well, not well at all. But his nurse seems to have given him a new lease of life. A shot in the arm. I do hope it's heroin. It shortens one's days, and makes the nights bearable. I loathe the dark, dirty night.

CONRAD. I know.

GABRIEL. Then where were you last night to comfort me the way she did with her stories? I don't know all her secrets yet, but she is revealing herself to me. Near as I am to opening night – or closing, if you prefer – my dear Conrad, you'll be glad I at last have learned your director's patience. I'm learning from the way she sings, the clothes – always the clothes – that are part of her denial. And perhaps she is right to deny herself something. There is a hardness in her that is quite becoming. Like myself, she can turn to stone. No man will ever carve a madonna out of her. She does not yet know the reason for this, and she may never accept it, but the reason is herself, herself alone. If I had to play her, I believe I might be able, for she is her own man, or she will be eventually.

CONRAD. Are you in love with her?

GABRIEL. A dying man looks at a woman and sees his own reflection. That's not love. It's perversity. And yet I am not perverse. I was a good son, a good brother – ask Kassie. And to you, what was I?

(**CONRAD** *goes to kiss* **GABRIEL**. *He spurns him.*)

Don't come near me. Keep your hands to yourself. Don't touch me.

CONRAD. I have no intention of touching you.

GABRIEL. God's curse on the day you first did.

CONRAD. Do you believe in God?

GABRIEL. I believe in his mother. And that is a lie. I have never done anything but lie to you. You believed me.

CONRAD. Why did you lie?

GABRIEL. You left me –

CONRAD. Never.

GABRIEL. You left our house – our home – our bed. You left me for my flesh and blood, the young man who will inherit. You couldn't wait. You lacked patience. You let yourself down. You betrayed me. Before I die I will do the same. Betray you in Salamanca with a young priest begging the mother of God for intercession that he be forgiven for the sins that stain his vestments. Betray you in Elsinore walking through its haunted corridors waiting to devour the violent soldier who dressed me as Hamlet. In the climb between Florence and Fiesole where the Italian sun fries the air like butter I will do unto you sweating like a pig beneath me what you did to me.

CONRAD. I never lied to nor hated you. I've never betrayed you.

GABRIEL. A million times in your looks at other men.

CONRAD. If a man looks at me, do I look away –

GABRIEL. He looks at you with revulsion.

CONRAD. As you do. As you always have.

GABRIEL. Weeping – weeping – who is weeping, Conrad?

CONRAD. You are.

GABRIEL. I am very tired.

CONRAD. You're not well.

GABRIEL. Not well at all.

(silence)

CONRAD. Are you capable of seeing visitors tomorrow?

GABRIEL. Who is coming to pay homage?

CONRAD. Your sister.

GABRIEL. Her son?

CONRAD. Yes.

GABRIEL. My dear sister, Kassie. A tonic for the nerves. How I look forward to hearing her latest litany of physical and mental ailments. I do believe the only medical condition she has not suffered from is the harelip of the Hapsburgs. I'm sure she is working on it as we speak.

CONRAD. Will you see Ryan?

GABRIEL. Will he see me?

(silence)

That boy is a mystery to me. Why should he consent to sleep with you? Is he into necrophilia? How much did you pay him? Ah well, in that respect, he continues in his father's footsteps. I do hope you'll make sure we have money in the house. Just for him. Slip it to him when nobody's looking. Down the front of his open-neck shirt. Feel the warmth of his neck that leads to the rest of his beautifully perfumed body. I'm so glad he turned out good-looking – for your sake.

(silence)

Forgive me – I do hate hurting you, but you started it.

CONRAD. How?

GABRIEL. You loved me. You all love me. What a mistake, yes?

(silence)

No.

CONRAD. Perhaps.

(GABRIEL sings.)

GABRIEL. Falling in love again
   Never wanted to,
   What am I to do,
   I can't help it.

(Silence. GABRIEL and CONRAD laugh.)

Is there money in the house?

CONRAD. Yes.

GABRIEL. Enough?

CONRAD. There's always enough.

GABRIEL. Then I'll look forward to seeing them tomorrow. I do hope I last. Don't suffocate me as you leave. My Desdemona days are long past. I still know something about jealousy. Am I not quite the wronged wife?

(There is an intense light on the portrait in the living room.)

GABRIEL. *(cont.)* Surprise me.

(silence)

Make me laugh.

(silence)

Do you love me?

(silence)

Do you hate me?

CONRAD. I know you.

GABRIEL. You surprise me.

Scene Three

(GABRIEL sits out of bed, on a chair, in a dressing gown. ALMA sits on the bed. GABRIEL's sister, KASSIE, stands in the bedroom. CONRAD stands in the living room, a drink in his hand. RYAN, GABRIEL's nephew, sits on the couch, also drinking.)

KASSIE. Kenya. That's what it reminds me of. The smell in this room. The smell of Africa. Isn't that extraordinary?

CONRAD. Would you like another drink?

RYAN. If I did, I'd help myself.

KASSIE. I went there with my son, Ryan, for his twenty-first. A gift from Gabriel and Conrad. The Masai are the most beautiful people in the world. So tall, so black.

RYAN. So, he's still here.

KASSIE. But there was a definite smell. It hit you getting off the plane.

RYAN. Bravo, Gabriel.

CONRAD. Yes. Bravo.

KASSIE. The same smell as in here.

ALMA. Maybe it's me.

KASSIE. How could it be you? Nurses are known for their insistence on hygiene.

GABRIEL. Well, I've been washed, fed and watered. It's not me.

CONRAD. You're looking well, Ryan.

RYAN. You're looking – looking like yourself.

KASSIE. There's always a smell before a saint dies. A scent of roses. Or is that afterwards? I can't recall. Anyway, that's a load of nonsense. You certainly aren't a saint, Gabriel.

GABRIEL. Am I not, Kassie?

KASSIE. And you're not dying. Tell me, do you think there will be theatres in hell?

GABRIEL. Really, Kassandra.

KASSIE. In heaven. I meant to say in heaven. My mind's going astray. Is your mind going astray, Gabriel?

(**KASSIE** *starts to sniff. She takes out a handkerchief from her bag.*)

GABRIEL. That's right. Have a good cry. Have a really good cry. That will make us all feel much better.

CONRAD. Are you going in to see him today?

RYAN. Later – when we're leaving.

ALMA. Will you not sit down?

KASSIE. No, I won't sit down.

CONRAD. He does want to see you.

KASSIE. I never sit down in a sick room.

RYAN. I will see him. When I'm ready, when he's dying.

KASSIE. It's one of my superstitions.

ALMA. I never heard of that one.

KASSIE. I made it up myself. That's the kind of us as a family. Always inventive. Always different. Ryan, he's exactly the same. He takes after us entirely. Always on the go. Energetic. Difficult.

GABRIEL. Dangerous.

KASSIE. Just as you were. You're jealous because he's younger. He was always jealous of young people. Stop looking down your nose on your own nephew. What are you? An actor. What do you know about work?

ALMA. What do you do yourself, Kassie?

KASSIE. A professional poker player. Now retired. I was great at bluffing. But the nerves go as you get older. Still, I've no regrets. It was a great chance to travel the world. I was known by name in Las Vegas. Everyone called me Sylvia.

ALMA. I thought your name was Kassie?

KASSIE. It is. Sometimes.

CONRAD. Have you set eyes recently –

RYAN. On my father? Yes, I visit him in the hostel.

KASSIE. Are you married, Alma?

ALMA. I'm not, no, Kassie.

CONRAD. No better?

RYAN. Still sick with drink. Still asking about you.

KASSIE. You should marry. Being alone is terrible.

RYAN. I always lie and tell him you remember him.

CONRAD. I do remember him.

RYAN. I invent little details to please him. Tell him you still think he had the makings of the best actor in your company. That brings a smile to his face. You wouldn't recognise his face now.

ALMA. Is your husband –

KASSIE. Still alive, the father of my child? Yes, but he did a runner. He walked out of a Chinese restaurant and I never saw him again. We were sharing a plate of prawns.

GABRIEL. Maybe they disagreed with him.

KASSIE. It did surprise me when he ordered them. He was never a great man for the fish.

CONRAD. Your father made a balls of his life.

RYAN. Did he, Conrad? I know everything.

KASSIE. To my own credit, I did try to get him back. I tried to track him down.

RYAN. He was blackmailed into marrying her.

KASSIE. This town was smaller then. I did find the dump of a flat he was hiding in.

RYAN. She did the blackmailing. She said she'd name him and her own brother as homosexuals, she'd go to the police.

KASSIE. I knocked at his door – no answer.

RYAN. And to save your skin, you let her marry him.

KASSIE. So I did what any decent woman would do.

GABRIEL. You hurled a brick through his window.

ALMA. Why did you do that?

KASSIE. A romantic gesture that went awry. The bastard threw the brick back. It missed my head by inches. Somebody must have been praying for me. This time it was me did the runner.

RYAN. Twice in the past five years he's tried to drown himself.

KASSIE. Is my brother eating? Is he managing a bit of chicken when he's sick? Chicken's very good when your stomach is upset.

RYAN. Yes, I'm sure you'd not recognize his face now. He looks as if he's swallowed the ocean. I'll take that drink now. Have one yourself. Keep me company.

KASSIE. I always pray for you, Gabriel.

GABRIEL. And I pray for you.

(**CONRAD** *pours drinks.*)

KASSIE. If anything happens to you, I'll die.

GABRIEL. Nothing is going to happen.

KASSIE. It's just that last night I heard the banshee wailing.

(*She starts to sniff again.*)

GABRIEL. Go ahead, Kassie. Keep the banshee company.

RYAN. I'd like some money.

CONRAD. What for?

RYAN. Services rendered. An old debt. For my father. Have you poured me a drink?

(**CONRAD** *pours the drink on to the floor.*)

CONRAD. Pour it yourself.

RYAN. I will.

CONRAD. I think I do recognize your father. You grow more like him.

RYAN. I always was. That's why you liked me.

ALMA. Do you believe that crap about the banshee?

GABRIEL. She knows that I do.

KASSIE. Our family always has. Before a death, first there's knock on the door. Then the banshee wailing. To be honest with you, I'm overreacting to last night. There was no knock at the door.

GABRIEL. That's a comfort.

KASSIE. I thought it would be. That's why I told you.

(GABRIEL *bursts out laughing.*)

GABRIEL. Kassie, I believe you.

KASSIE. Why should you not? I'm your sister. Jesus, Alma, the time we had as children. It was so beautiful to grow up in Salamanca.

ALMA. You were born there?

KASSIE. No – no. We were born in Argentina. We moved there as children. What age were we? I can't remember. But I do remember the servants and the smell of yellow bread baking. There were always prawns in the kitchen, pink and big as your fist. And tiny birds you stuck a fork into and blood shot out from between their bones. There was rice to eat, milky rice with the fragrance of spinach, all green floating through the white. I loved Spain. I must go there some day.

ALMA. You've never been?

KASSIE. Only as a child, and from what Gabriel's told me. That's how I remember. I believe what I remember.

RYAN. Is Gabriel really dying?

GABRIEL. You see, Alma, we believe in what we're told. The two of us. We always have. I think that's why I became an actor. I believe lies.

KASSIE. Because they're not.

CONRAD. He has an aneurism on his heart. It could burst at any minute.

ALMA. Is that not a dangerous way to live?

RYAN. His heart?

KASSIE. I learned one thing playing cards – all life is danger.

CONRAD. His heart.

GABRIEL. Alma's life isn't.

(KASSIE *sits on the bed beside* ALMA.)

RYAN. Can nothing be done?

GABRIEL. She's allergic to it.

KASSIE. To danger?

GABRIEL. To life. But not to death. That's why she nurses the dying.

(ALMA *rises from the bed.*)

KASSIE. I've often wondered where people find that kind of courage.

CONRAD. He has bowel cancer. In its early stages.

GABRIEL. Is it courage, Alma? Would you call it courage?

ALMA. I don't like the turn this conversation is taking.

CONRAD. They can do nothing to heal one without ensuring the other will kill him.

(*silence*)

If our prayers are answered, it will be his heart. Quicker. A shock, a savage one, but swift – no excess of pain. Not for him that's gone. Those left behind will die in some way too. Me, your mother – and you as well, Ryan. We will be spared one sight, though. He won't grow too old and be caged away for that crime against nature. He might be, as I would be, disruptive. They'd tie him down. He'd be fed, washed and watered, then –

RYAN. He would be left to die. The way my father has been left –

ALMA. Let me remind the two of you that I'm a stranger. I'm here to do my job. And I do it well. Very well. I may not be a big shot in the theatre. I may not have made a fortune playing poker.

KASSIE. Maybe I never touched a hand of poker in my life.

ALMA. You told me –

KASSIE. You believed me?

ALMA. Does madness run in your family?

KASSIE. Our mother had a saying. Sanity is like your fanny. Hold on to it.

CONRAD. Are you telling me you love your father?

ALMA. I think you are both very unkind. You play bad games with each other and with other people.

CONRAD. Is that his latest torture?

ALMA. I know how to play those games. They are played by cruel children. I am not a child, and I am not cruel.

CONRAD. Your father does not love you. He loves the price of the next drink. The only thing he values is money – money he spends on himself. He's never wasted a penny on you. He does not love you. And I say that for his benefit as much as yours. That is truly for services rendered. He does not love you.

RYAN. And you do?

(silence)

ALMA. I was not let be what I wanted to be.

GABRIEL. What did you want to be?

ALMA. A fucking professional poker player in Las Vegas. Someone who lost her money on the last throw of the dice. She goes to blow her brains out with a silver pistol in the back seat of a blue sports car and just when she's about to do it, just when she feels the beautifully cold metal against her sweating skin, she doesn't do it because she has a son. To die would be to sentence him to the mercy of his father. His lost, lousy father.

KASSIE. She believes, Gabriel. Where did she get it from?

GABRIEL. Alma has a dead brother. Sometimes he takes possession of her. She enjoys that danger.

ALMA. Possession?

GABRIEL. Possession.

ALMA. I am all my own work.

GABRIEL. You are your brother's sister.

KASSIE. That's a close bond, darling. Were they lovers?

GABRIEL. They were twins.

KASSIE. We were neither, so we can't comment.

ALMA. He was my soul. He's dead.

KASSIE. My brother's dying.

GABRIEL. She admits it.

(KASSIE *stretches out on the bed.*)

KASSIE. This is a grand comfortable bed.

RYAN. Why do you say he tortures me? My father?

CONRAD. I am well versed in your family's addiction.

RYAN. To drink?

CONRAD. To suffering.

RYAN. And I want the same suffering? I want to punish myself for being my parents' son? You believe that history repeats itself? I know you were a glutton for punishment, Conrad. And you are a fool as well if you think my mother and my father rule the roost over my life.

GABRIEL. Get off the bed, Kassie.

RYAN. Because they failed, it doesn't mean I fail.

KASSIE. Stretch out here –

GABRIEL. Get off our bed.

RYAN. I am trying hard not to fail.

KASSIE. I'll curl about your feet, your feet and Conrad's feet – like a cat.

RYAN. And you failed, both of you. Gabriel and Conrad failed.

(KASSIE *sits up on the bed. She disturbs the bedclothes, using her fingers like claws.*)

CONRAD. Yes, we did.

GABRIEL. Stop.

CONRAD. Failed.

KASSIE. I'll creep into your bed.

RYAN. You'll leave nothing behind you.

CONRAD. We leave a theatre.

RYAN. That nobody wants.

KASSIE. You won't know I'm there, Gabriel. I'll steal Conrad.

CONRAD. It's yours if you want it.

RYAN. I want something different.

KASSIE. I could destroy you if I wanted to.

RYAN. You're not my father. Neither of you.

KASSIE. You remember that.

RYAN. You have no children. I am my father's child. He did more than you did.

KASSIE. I'll outlast you. Because I have a family.

GABRIEL. Yes, my dear, the family. Our family.

KASSIE. Our mother kept us locked up like china. Don't climb trees, you'll break your neck. Don't swim in that water, you'll drown. Don't talk to your father, he's drunk, dirty, dangerous. He'll touch me.

GABRIEL. And I'll die. I think that's what my death will be like. My father touching me, and telling me I'm his son. Is that how your brother died?

ALMA. Why have I come here to nurse you?

RYAN. Can I come to see Gabriel soon?

ALMA. How do you know me?

GABRIEL. Because you've told me.

CONRAD. It might be a mercy if you didn't.

ALMA. Told you what?

GABRIEL. What I need to know – before I die.

RYAN. Mercy for who? Me?

(silence)

KASSIE. Well, Gabriel, I leave you in good hands. She's a match for you. And she's as beautiful as you were when you were younger. So don't be jealous. Alma, I can walk away from my brother a happy woman.

GABRIEL. Thank you for calling.

KASSIE. I've had a bad pain in my arm this past few weeks.

RYAN. I think my mother is very ill.

KASSIE. They say it's a sign of the heart breaking.

RYAN. If Gabriel dies she won't last long.

CONRAD. Yes, I think that's right.

KASSIE. I'll have to pray to St. Bernadette.

GABRIEL. Kassie, please stop.

KASSIE. Our mother took Bernadette for her Confirmation name. She must have looked lovely making her Confirmation. My brother is the image of her.

GABRIEL. Kassie, take me to the pictures. You and me and mother going to the pictures.

KASSIE. She loved Jennifer Jones. That was because she played the saint in *The Song of Bernadette.*

GABRIEL. For those who do not believe –

KASSIE. No explanation is possible.

GABRIEL. For those who do believe –

KASSIE. No explanation is necessary.

ALMA. And you two believe anything.

RYAN. I don't know what to do.

ALMA. You believe in God.

CONRAD. Then there's two of us.

ALMA. You believe in his mother.

(**RYAN** *kisses* **CONRAD.**)

RYAN. Why do you always show me mercy?

ALMA. And you're in for a rude awakening.

RYAN. Why do you always forgive me?

CONRAD. Because you never do anything to be forgiven.

GABRIEL. Kassie, don't leave me.

KASSIE. I'll never leave you.

CONRAD. Pour your mother a drink. She'll need one.

(**RYAN** *does so.*)

GABRIEL. Don't let me die.

KASSIE. Gabriel, Mother died, Father died.

CONRAD. Pour one for me and one for yourself.

RYAN. I'm all right – I'm driving.

KASSIE. We all die, you and me –

GABRIEL. But we were children –

KASSIE. We grow up.

GABRIEL. No, we don't.

KASSIE. I'm afraid we do, darling. We do.

ALMA. And we die.

Scene Four

(Later evening, the bedroom in soft, golden light. In bed,
GABRIEL *sits propped up with pillows.* **CONRAD** *smokes*
a long pipe. **ALMA** *sits in candlelight in the living room.)*

GABRIEL. I do wish at your age you would stop smoking laudanum.

CONRAD. You're taking morphine.

GABRIEL. Mine is medicinal.

CONRAD. So is mine.

GABRIEL. How so?

CONRAD. I take it for a condition that has long troubled me.

GABRIEL. What is that?

CONRAD. Enduring you.

GABRIEL. I have now turned into an endurance.

CONRAD. You are a painted tart.

GABRIEL. Bitch. A tart, yes. Painted never. When I went to Kenya as a young man, on my twenty-first birthday, the Masai women worshipped me as a god. They saw a fire of gold around my white flesh. They called me Apollo.

CONRAD. No, dear, they called you Daphne – or whatever the Masai equivalent is.

GABRIEL. You always turn nasty on laudanum. And you look vaguely Japanese smoking that pipe.

CONRAD. I think you mean Chinese, don't you?

GABRIEL. I know the difference between those races. I did spend a considerable amount of time in both countries. My Japanese colleagues could not believe I was not a native when I was training for the Kabuki. They may have been right, for I feel my soul is oriental. My grace playing the female roles convinced them I was steeped in their tradition.

CONRAD. Did you wear the conventional long black wig?

GABRIEL. No, I used my own hair.

CONRAD. Oh good, then you got laughs.

GABRIEL. When did it happen?

CONRAD. What?

GABRIEL. When did we turn into bickering fools? Was it when we grew old? Or were we always like this?

CONRAD. I don't think so.

GABRIEL. Nor do I. Maybe that's the morphine talking.

CONRAD. Are you in pain?

GABRIEL. Why do you ask that?

CONRAD. You might need –

GABRIEL. More? Are you trying to kill me? I would put nothing past you. You come close to it at work. Demanding more. Always more. And when there is nothing left to demand –

CONRAD. Then I ask you to do more, but do it less obviously.

GABRIEL. Was I that obvious? I suppose so. A fitting epitaph. My director tells me, tells me on my deathbed, that my life, my career, my art – all obvious. A child of ten could have done it better. I did start acting at the age of ten. Perhaps if you had got your hands on me at the age of ten you could have corrupted me into something more subtle. Fuck subtlety and fuck you. There is something I have been longing especially to tell you for an absolute age. You could not direct my cock out of a paper bag.

CONRAD. If you have ever positioned your cock into a paper bag I might have been of some help. However, you never did. It usually travelled into more predictable locations. Was there a taxi driver in this city who didn't taste your tongue?

GABRIEL. There were two I resisted.

CONRAD. Why?

GABRIEL. Presbyterians. Even I had my limits. They were good, clean country boys, but I could smell the Bible through their trousers. And it wasn't the wedding feast at Cana.

CONRAD. You shock me.

GABRIEL. That I resisted?

CONRAD. That there are Presbyterians driving taxis.

GABRIEL. That trade is a broad church.

CONRAD. You never brought any home, did you?

GABRIEL. Never.

CONRAD. I did. They knew the inside of the house remarkably well.

GABRIEL. Many of them are psychic. A broad church, as I say. Perhaps I should have been a taxi driver.

CONRAD. Perhaps you should have been a Presbyterian.

GABRIEL. Or a psychic, like John of Gaunt.

(He quotes –)

'Methinks I am a prophet new inspired,
And thus expiring do foretell of him:
His rash, fierce, blaze of riot cannot last,
For violent fires soon burn out themselves.'

(silence)

CONRAD. Well remembered.

GABRIEL. You really should have cast me as John of Gaunt. He's dead and off the stage before the first hour. Instead I had to hoof on as Richard II. I was too old to play it when I did.

CONRAD. You were twenty-five.

GABRIEL. That young – really – when I played it? Was I good – was I – was I – obvious? Yes, that's the word I'm looking for. No, maybe I was better than that. Perhaps I was adequate. Your highest praise. I do believe if you had attended the first night of *The Magic Flute* you would have looked at Mozart and said, 'Thank you, Wolfgang darling, that was adequate.'

CONRAD. It is.

GABRIEL. I know. You have a good ear.

CONRAD. You have a good eye.

GABRIEL. I can run up a frock, paint a set, write a good line, and I know how to act.

CONRAD. Yes, you do.

GABRIEL. Are you sure?

CONRAD. I'm certain.

GABRIEL. Then will we take a risk? Start a company?

CONRAD. Start a theatre?

GABRIEL. We're young enough, we'll do work that no one else does, the great Europeans, new plays the like of which this country – this city –

CONRAD. We shall turn this town into –

GABRIEL. A new Athens?

CONRAD. I was thinking of Sodom.

GABRIEL. That's more realistic.

CONRAD. We shall conceive a child in Sodom –

GABRIEL. Not a child, a place, a palace, and we shall open the windows and the doors and the gates that lead –

CONRAD. To this, our theatre.

(silence)

GABRIEL. So long ago.

CONRAD. We did do it.

GABRIEL. I'm frightened.

CONRAD. Of what we're doing?

GABRIEL. Of what we've done.

CONRAD. Don't be. I'm beside you.

GABRIEL. That's precisely why I am frightened. Of you, beside me. Of what we've done together. I may go to hell in a wheelbarrow because of it. Pain. I need more morphine.

CONRAD. I'll get Alma.

GABRIEL. I'm in pain.

CONRAD. Please be calm.

GABRIEL. Pain.

CONRAD. How can I help you?

GABRIEL. Pain.

CONRAD. Is it bearable?

GABRIEL. Thank you, quite bearable. I'm so sorry, wasn't that obvious?

(silence)

Do finish your pipe, darling. I do hope I've not ruined your smoke. We painted tarts hate to disappoint.

*(**GABRIEL** throws away the wig from his head.)*

I do believe you're going to cry. Don't ever do that in my presence. If I do not cry, you will not. And stop feeding me dreams, because they sicken me even more than my malignant stomach does. They're past and gone, those dirty dreams. They're as ugly as I am.

*(From the living room **ALMA**'s voice is barely audible as she sings.)*

ALMA. No one believed what she had seen,
No one believed what she had heard,
That there were sorrows to be healed,
And mercy, mercy in this world.

CONRAD. You can act. I've never questioned that.

GABRIEL. Fetch my wig.

CONRAD. No.

(silence)

How did you remember John of Gaunt's lines? You never played it.

GABRIEL. You learned the whole play off by heart. So did I. You were standing always at the back of the theatre, mouthing every word, going through everything we were going through. I did the same. It was for you.

CONRAD. That was good of you.

GABRIEL. I had an eye to the future, as always. Someday I might have played John of Gaunt.

CONRAD. Someday you still might.

GABRIEL. Are you offering me the part?

CONRAD. No.

GABRIEL. Fiend. Fiend from hell.

CONRAD. You flatter me.

GABRIEL. I suppose I do. You enjoy that? You would prefer hell to heaven?

CONRAD. I am too tired for metaphysics.

GABRIEL. As I am.

CONRAD. Then sleep.

GABRIEL. I wish I could.

CONRAD. You'll sleep like a baby.

GABRIEL. Babies.

> *(silence)*

Do you regret –

CONRAD. No.

GABRIEL. You didn't want a child?

CONRAD. Perhaps. What point wanting now?

GABRIEL. Who knows how it would have turned out?

CONRAD. Disastrously.

GABRIEL. Inevitably. Sad, isn't it?

CONRAD. No, not remotely.

GABRIEL. I'm thinking of the child that might have been. A sad character. A misplaced person. Friendless, and so inclined to talk to itself. Mocked by other children. Possessing a good mind, but really not of this world, and never ready for the next, a boy rare as lapis lazuli.

CONRAD. I think I would have liked such a child.

GABRIEL. Good, because I gave him to you. I gave you my life.

CONRAD. That was kind of you, but you should have mentioned it before.

GABRIEL. Didn't I?

CONRAD. Not within my hearing.

GABRIEL. You told me not to shout. Always your note. Don't shout.

CONRAD. And a good note it was.

GABRIEL. I'm so glad you're certain.

CONRAD. I am.

GABRIEL. I am tired now. Turn out the lamp.

CONRAD. I shall dim it.

GABRIEL. Let us away, let us away
  Now the wild white horses play,
  Champ, chafe and toss in the spray,
  Children dear, let us away.

(CONRAD *dims the light in the bedroom.* RYAN *lights a lamp in the sitting room.* ALMA *starts on the couch.*)

ALMA. Where the hell did you come from?

RYAN. I think you've a fucking good idea.

ALMA. Did you break into the house?

RYAN. This is mine. I inherit it. Sorry to disappoint you, but that's settled. You know my mother. She's met you. We know all about your plans. Dying old men, that's who you're after. We've been warned about you. Sorry, sister, you've picked the wrong family.

ALMA. Jesus, you've caught me.

RYAN. You admit it?

ALMA. That I kill old people? Of course.

RYAN. Are you trying to be funny?

ALMA. No. They give their life into my hands, and I strangle them. If they're too tough for that, I poison them. I take their money and beat them over the head with a stick until their blood –

RYAN. Don't mention blood –

ALMA. Are you afraid of blood? All right, no sign of blood. I can do it with a scarf. With my bare hands. But before we go into the intimate details of murder, who are you? I've guessed, you're family.

RYAN. My mother and myself have decided. You're not needed. I can be his nurse. I can stay here and –

ALMA. Watch him dying.

RYAN. He's not going to die. I can take care of him. He will survive. I can nurse him.

ALMA. He's going to die. It will be soon. You can do nothing for him. And I will be with him.

RYAN. You want his money.

ALMA. There's not much there. You've seen to that.

RYAN. They owe me. They owe my mother.

ALMA. They owe the two of you nothing.

RYAN. We don't need their money.

ALMA. But you still ask for it.

RYAN. I do, because she doesn't. She doesn't know how to look after herself.

ALMA. You do. That must be a comfort.

RYAN. If it is, what concern of yours? You don't belong here. I don't need to defend myself to you. We want you out of the house. Now, if necessary. Tomorrow at the latest.

ALMA. How can you do that?

RYAN. There are ways.

ALMA. Are you threatening me?

RYAN. I love Gabriel. I should look after him.

ALMA. But you can't. You're not trained.

RYAN. How do you know?

ALMA. You studied medicine, didn't you? Oh Jesus, of course – bright boy, but you didn't last the course. It didn't matter, though. You'd be looked after anyway.

RYAN. No, wrong – completely wrong. Where you got that idea God knows. I hadn't the brains for that. Just like yourself. But I do hope you're clever enough to know where you're not wanted. Leave.

ALMA. No.

RYAN. We'll see about that.

ALMA. We'll see.

RYAN. If anything happens to Gabriel, I will hold you responsible.

ALMA. You're a frightened boy.

RYAN. I mean it.

ALMA. You can't stop him dying.

RYAN. Watch me.

ALMA. I will. Do you live on your own?

RYAN. Why do you want to know?

ALMA. I hope you do. You always will. I'll leave when I'm ready. When he's left this world. Goodnight.

RYAN. I'm warning you.

ALMA. I'm breaking my heart.

RYAN. I mean it.

ALMA. You might. Who knows? Who cares?

RYAN. Gabriel does. About me.

ALMA. Yes, they all do. For no discernible reason, other than you're theirs. Lucky man.

RYAN. Very. Sometimes.

ALMA. Most times, I'd say.

RYAN. It will last, my luck.

ALMA. It never does. Don't drink and drive.

RYAN. I don't.

ALMA. I believe you. Goodnight.

RYAN. I'll be back. *(He leaves.)*

ALMA. You'll come back. No doubt. And I'll be here. So will he. Waiting. For a while.

Scene Five

(In the bedroom **ALMA** *is about to shave* **GABRIEL**, *who has still discarded his wig.)*

ALMA. I've always envied men – shaving. It must be lovely. A woman has hair on her lip – it's a travesty. A man – it's natural. Jesus, I hate nature.

GABRIEL. I adore nature. Men tend to, as we grow older. Some men take to gardening in a passionate way. Their love life centres on their lobelias. Others, like myself, retain their sanity. No, I will go out praising the natural world. I have been practising my last words. They're quite perfect now. They shall be, 'I long for the sea.'

ALMA. You're a man who loves the sea.

GABRIEL. Certainly not. I would not set foot in that filth. I'm simply thinking of dying as I have lived. An enigma. The sea is far too unruly for me. Far too female. And yet perhaps I should have loved it more. Perhaps I should have made love to a woman.

ALMA. You never did?

GABRIEL. In my day one didn't. It wasn't considered quite right for a young man in my sexual situation. But I've always thought it must be terribly sweet to have a girlfriend. For me, she would be pale, pale as the moon in some severe Victorian painting condemning female passion, so she would dislike passion. I would be adored for my restraint. Then she would break my heart and marry someone else. They always do, women. Marry rather rowdy medical students, safe in the blissful ignorance I'd fucked their future husbands. Dear God, how many men have I scared into the arms of women? I shudder to think. If Dr. Freud were still dwelling amongst us, the poor darling would have me diagnosed as the cause of heterosexuality.

ALMA. Wishful thinking there, sunshine.

*(**ALMA** continues shaving **GABRIEL**.)*

GABRIEL. You do remind me of a girl I once acted with. She was Jessica to my Shylock.

ALMA. You've lost me there.

GABRIEL. Jessica betrays her Jewish father, Shylock. My Jessica was a girl of exceptional beauty. She acted well. She defied me, on stage. Quite right, of course, that was her role. Jessica must defy Shylock. I believed in her. I never forgave her. Conrad adored her. Her beauty reminded him of mine. When the play ended, I never saw her again. It is sometimes best to be rid of people. You can never be too ruthless. You must always be capable of killing. Are you a killer, Alma?

(He grabs **ALMA***'s hand with the razor and holds it against his throat.)*

You could kill me now. Slice my throat. You could place the blade in my mouth. Carve the tongue away. I have the physical power still to make you do that. A man can take a woman's hand and force her to commit an act of violence. I can make you move this weapon down between my legs and cut my cock away, cut it clean – make me clean – make me not a man – is that what a woman wants?

*(***RYAN*** enters the living room on his way to the bedroom. He listens.)*

ALMA. How would you know what a woman wants? How would any man know?

*(***GABRIEL*** releases* **ALMA***'s hand.)*

GABRIEL. Tell me.

ALMA. Sometimes they want to be us. I believe that frightens men. You turn that fear into hate. Or maybe it's love. Stop asking what women want. They won't tell you. Wonder instead what men want. I know. It's what they can't have. If they did, they'd stop being men, and they wouldn't want that, for they always want more.

GABRIEL. More – the car crash – tell me more.

ALMA. Tell you what? Perhaps that night was possessed. I know he was behind the wheel. I know there was another car coming. Perhaps we didn't see it. Perhaps he didn't want to. The traffic lights went red. Or maybe they were green. I don't know. You can't blame me for that. I'm told his death was instantaneous. I'm told I did not say a word. When I did speak, I believe I roared, 'My brother is dead.' Or perhaps it was a whisper. I could have been accusing myself, for it's possible I was not in the car with him and if I was, did I leave him to die, get rid of him, quite ruthlessly? Was I, in fact, his killer? *(She puts the razor to her own throat.)* You said my brother possessed me. No, it's you he's after and he's found you. But I'll outlast both you fuckers. You can't kill me. Only I can do that to myself.

GABRIEL. What are you going to do?

(She throws the razor on to the bed.)

Continue shaving me.

(She does so.)

ALMA. You're nursing me well.

GABRIEL. It's a vocation.

ALMA. When did you know you had it?

GABRIEL. Some years ago – many years ago – there was a joke circulating in this town. The University had given me an honorary doctorate. Services to theatre. Conrad was furious. You've never seen him in a fury.

ALMA. He's the mildest of men.

GABRIEL. Would the mildest of men have lasted this long with me?

ALMA. No.

GABRIEL. Then I will continue my story. The phone never stopped ringing. The entire world seemed to be celebrating. Or so I thought, but I digress. Conrad received all these messages of goodwill on my behalf. I had developed a sudden allergy to telephone receivers. 'Well deserved, tell Doctor Gabriel.' 'This is long

GABRIEL. *(cont.)* overdue, tell Doctor Gabriel.' 'Warmest congratulations to Doctor Gabriel.' It really was too much for the poor darling. He finally snapped and said, 'I'm afraid Doctor Gabriel is not available at the moment for consultation, will Nurse Conrad do?' Since that day I have always admired nurses.

(RYAN is now near the bedroom. He carries a large bag of oranges.)

ALMA. I don't believe there's a bad bone in that man's body.

GABRIEL. His body.

(silence)

I know that body. Every smell, every sense, every inch. The body that's betrayed mine.

ALMA. How has he betrayed you?

GABRIEL. By loving me. Loving this rotting carcass.

(RYAN has entered his bedroom.)

A dying animal.

RYAN. You're not. That is not going to happen. I won't let it happen.

(silence)

GABRIEL. Yes, it is.

RYAN. Why are you giving up? You never shied away from a fight. You're a brave man. Don't lie down –

GABRIEL. Like a dying animal, a rotting carcass.

RYAN. Stop saying that. Look, I've been asking around. You can't believe everything doctors tell you. You can't. There are other kinds of medicine. You have to try anything. There's ways of getting your health back. *(He pours oranges in a cascade over the bed.)* You can be healed. Boil these and drink the liquid left after. Do that three times a day. Dozens of oranges – I'll come with them. Hundreds of oranges. Boil them. Vitamin C – buckets of it. Drink it. They eat up the dying cells – it's a cure –

GABRIEL. Alma, tell him what good that will do.

ALMA. He may as well stick his head up a horse's arse.

GABRIEL. I may have done so when I was drunk. I do hope the horse enjoyed it, but I'm not tempted to repeat the experience.

RYAN. I'll try anything to save you.

(RYAN *starts to weep quietly. He turns his back. His weeping grows violent.*)

GABRIEL. You're a good fellow to try and save me. You can't. It would be easier to climb the Matterhorn in high heels, and only I have accomplished that. I no longer have the energy, my dear.

(*The weeping has stopped.*)

You've now stopped your remarkably accurate impersonation of Greer Garson. You may sit beside me.

(GABRIEL *nods to* ALMA. *She leads* RYAN *to the bed. He sits beside* GABRIEL. *They do not touch.* ALMA *gathers up the oranges.*)

I insisted on knowing what was going to happen to me. When they told me, do you know what I did? I wept like you did. Exactly like you. That is how frightened I am. Do you believe me?

RYAN. Yes.

GABRIEL. I'm leaving. This tends to happen to the men you love. It always will, if you persist in wanting revenge for your father.

RYAN. I'm not looking for that.

ALMA. What are you looking for?

RYAN. Who the hell are you to ask me that?

ALMA. You want him to love you. If he does, you'd blame him. That's your way to blackmail.

GABRIEL. For years being blackmailed was how we lived our lives. Myself and Conrad. You say, we never shied away from a fight, we were brave. No, that's not true. We could always expect a knock at the door or a letter – never posted for some reason, always hand-delivered

GABRIEL. *(cont.)* to our home. They would demand we do this, fix that, or else they would tell. 'Who and what are you going to tell?' I'd confront them. Do you know, they usually turned somewhat shy of going into detail? Their great threat was that they'd state the obvious. And that's what the police would have believed. The obvious. The details would be left purely to the imagination. I think that is really why they feared the two of us. We forced them to use their foul, fascinating imaginations. They liked that sufficiently to harm us as much as they could manage. They had to. We were dangerous. We were men who loved each other and lived together openly as lovers when it was a fucking crime to do so. How ludicrous, how cruel, how hard to believe now. But we were the truth and they hated us, and loved us, for being so. I let them. I accepted them. I forgave them. Paid them.

RYAN. You wanted to be hurt?

GABRIEL. You're one of the family, you must understand that.

RYAN. I don't want to hurt you.

GABRIEL. You're your father's son and your mother's child.

RYAN. I can be my own man.

GABRIEL. Prove it.

RYAN. Let me finish shaving you.

ALMA. Are you trying to do my job?

(**RYAN** *lifts the razor and shaves* **GABRIEL.**)

RYAN. I'm a bit nervous about cutting you. Do you always use blades?

ALMA. I'm talking to you.

RYAN. I'm trying to help.

ALMA. You're a hindrance. You're a waste of time in a sick room. You're useless, aren't you?

(*He ignores her.*)

Are you not going to answer me? Am I not here? I've seen you and your like before. What you see in you is what you get, but nobody gets back very much. Then you're gone, as if you never were. I know you. Crying to our mother – spoilt by our father. You turned them against me. They blamed me. They hated me for what happened to you. It was your fault. I blame you as they blamed me. Why have you come back to me?

RYAN. I've never met you before now.

ALMA. You died on me some years ago.

RYAN. I never set eyes on you till last night.

ALMA. You remind me –

RYAN. That's not my fault.

ALMA. Stop haunting me.

RYAN. How can I haunt you? I'm not dead.

ALMA. You're covered in blood, you who hate the sight of it.

RYAN. You hate the sight of yourself. Whoever you see, it's not me. Gabriel tell her who I am.

GABRIEL. Alma, this is my nephew. He's not your brother. He's not, and you know that.

ALMA. Yes. My brother's gone. He won't be coming back.

GABRIEL. No, he won't.

RYAN. How did you know I can't look at blood?

ALMA. Didn't you tell me?

RYAN. I can't remember.

ALMA. I can. You panic at the sight of it.

RYAN. No, it's the smell.

GABRIEL. When he was a boy, his nose bled during the night. He'd wake up, the pillow was drenched red. It scared him.

RYAN. I'm still afraid of it. I suppose I wouldn't be much use in a sickroom.

ALMA. You get used to it. You learn to hide it. I think you might be good at that.

GABRIEL. There's worse things than shedding blood.

RYAN. What?

GABRIEL. Breathing – not knowing if your next will be your last. Hearing your own breath, smelling it, foul, frightening you but not wanting it yet to stop. I don't want you here when that happens.

RYAN. I want to be here. I want to help you.

GABRIEL. You can by helping Alma. Promise me you will.

RYAN. If that's what you want.

GABRIEL. It is.

ALMA. You can fetch and carry, I presume. We need more shaving stuff. Lotions. And tissues. Lots of them. Man-size tissues.

RYAN. Is that all?

ALMA. Oranges. More oranges. I'll boil these up. He'll drink the liquid. We'll try anything. Won't we, Gabriel?

GABRIEL. Anything.

RYAN. You believe there's a chance it might work?

ALMA. You belong to this family, you believe anything, all of you. So why not try it?

RYAN. I'll be back soon.

(He kisses GABRIEL. *He exits.)*

ALMA. We'll never see him again.

GABRIEL. You will. I know that. You have him quite intrigued with this talk of haunting. He wants to know more. Just like a man. More. I am angry with myself about one thing. I dazzle the poor darling with my talk of telling the truth. And yet in one important particular I've told him a lie. When I was told that I was dying, I didn't weep the way he's just done. Not my way. I opened my throat and I screamed.

(silence)

As if I were giving birth, I screamed.

Scene Six

(CONRAD and KASSIE play cards at a small table in the candlelit living room. The game is pontoon. GABRIEL lies asleep in the near-darkened bedroom. KASSIE throws a coin toward CONRAD. They each have a pile of coins beside them.)

KASSIE. Do you know why I love you?

CONRAD. You do?

KASSIE. You're a peacemaker.

(CONRAD deals the cards. They look at their hands. KASSIE nods. He deals her another card. She throws the hand down. She throws a coin to CONRAD.)

Blessed are the peacemakers. Yes, blessed Conrad. That's the first step to becoming a saint. Or is it venerable?

(He deals another hand. This time KASSIE wins. CONRAD throws her a coin.)

The Venerable Bede. When I was seriously gambling, I used to pray to him. To hell with St. Anthony – too many other clients. Myself and Bede, we were strictly monogamous.

CONRAD. But why this devotion to the Venerable Bede?

KASSIE. His monastery was in Jarrow, in the north of England. When I was a girl growing up there, I loved the story of the men marching from Jarrow to London, the hunger march, looking for justice. That fantasy. They were true socialists. My God, do you remember socialism? So do I. I'll never forget standing in front of the Committee of UnAmerican Affairs. Some weasel turned to me and asked, 'Are you now or have you ever been a member of the Communist Party?' I said, 'Of course I fucking am. Why do you think I'm standing here?'

(CONRAD deals another hand.)

CONRAD. You never were.

KASSIE. I suppose I wasn't. But I wish I were. It would have been the right thing to do at the time. I've never lacked courage. And courage is ridiculous. I am a ridiculous woman. Ridiculous to have loved you. Loved my husband. Any woman who loves a man leaves herself open to ridicule. They are only after one thing. Babies. Have a child, have my child. That's what they want.

(She checks her cards. She nods. He deals them both another card. She shows her hand. He throws her a coin.)

I should have had that baby. My son. When I had the abortion, when I lost my child –

CONRAD. You didn't lose him. He lived. He was here a few hours ago.

KASSIE. You are so perceptive. Yes, he did live. That was courageous of me. I wanted to get rid of him. You wouldn't let me.

CONRAD. I wasn't there. You made your own decision.

(She carefully pours two lines of cocaine on the table. She rolls up a banknote. She gives it to **CONRAD.** *He takes the line.)*

KASSIE. You helped me make it. Yes, you weren't there, but I could hear your whispering in my ear, you must go through with this birth, your child must be born, Gabriel and myself will protect you, the Party needs new blood –

CONRAD. I am not now and I have never been a member of the Communist Party.

KASSIE. Jesus, how could you betray the cause? But you do destroy people. You destroyed me and my husband. You are Stalin. You have betrayed me. Tonight I am the Venerable Rosa Luxemburg. That is who I am now. That is how I have died in mysterious circumstances.

CONRAD. You are not dead.

KASSIE. Possibly. *(She runs her finger along the line of cocaine.)*

CONRAD. Definitely.

KASSIE. I adore your certainty. I'm alive? *(She licks the cocaine.)*

CONRAD. Listen to yourself.

KASSIE. Do you?

CONRAD. I do nothing else. I hear your voice. I try to direct it into saying something I can reply to. So far, this evening –

KASSIE. I have succeeded in defying you. And I pride myself on that success. We share in making a small gesture of need. You need me to speak. I need you to listen. I can speak any nonsense you wish me to speak, and you will hear it. You see, that way we are still alive.

CONRAD. And we have not vanished entirely into our devouring love for your brother. Yes, I do listen to you, listen to him, to myself. And that is why I am alive.

KASSIE. Yes, I do love you very much.

CONRAD. You love your son.

KASSIE. I should love him.

CONRAD. And yet he will forget us all.

KASSIE. You blame him for that?

CONRAD. No. I have forgotten everything about what went before me. I am now forgetting everything that will come after me. I was once asked, 'What have you achieved in the theatre?' I replied, 'Nothing.' 'And what will you leave after you?' 'Well, the same, nothing.' The young man I gave those answers to, he was very angry with me, for he was planning to devote his life to this profession and he believed I was trying to destroy him. I wasn't. I was saving him. Or maybe I was seeing what he wanted, and he didn't like what I saw. For this was his beginning, his continuing, his end. He would, like myself, like yourself, turn into nothing, be not remembered and yet he would work with all his heart to prevent such forgetfulness. I believe in work. I am a hard-working man. That is how I have led my life, but where was it leading me? Nowhere? Perhaps. But that is immaterial. I work with all my strength to achieve – nothing. To leave nothing. That is what I

CONRAD. *(cont.)* have done and will never deny it. In that I am a man of a certain generation, a hard-liner – Stalin, you call me. But perhaps I belong to an earlier generation. I may be, like yourself, a follower of the Venerable Bede. Now there was a monk among monks. They were violent men. When the Vikings attacked, these holy men, chanting their *aves* to the goddess they loved, drew from the sleeves of their habits grenades, shotguns, knives and rifles. They blasted the bastards to kingdom come. Or so I believed, growing up as a boy, near Jarrow in the north of England.

KASSIE. You've never set foot in the place.

CONRAD. No more than you. But my point is this: if I have to have men about me, let them be warriors, that we may fight to the last for the sake of what we do and do not believe in, since there is no difference. We are men, all of us, and your brother proves it, he goes out, fighting.

KASSIE. And he has –

CONRAD. Not long left.

(silence)

Yes, not long left.

KASSIE. I've made my farewells.

CONRAD. From him?

KASSIE. You. Years ago. I sometimes wonder what it would have been like. You. No. I did what I did with my life. That does still make sense. I do know that woman who had to make up her own mind. She did, sitting in a hotel room in Piccadilly Circus where there was no room service, not even a bath, so she sat for hours on the bed, and though she didn't know, she was putting her lot into a pack of cards. *(She shuffles the cards expertly.)* This time she didn't have to bluff. She kept her nerve. For once she won. Her child takes after her. After her family. They do what they have to do very well. Fuck them all that tried to get rid of us. We survived. And my brother is the same. He'll survive.

(silence)

KASSIE. *(cont.)* I'll never see him again.

(silence)

That would be for the best.

CONRAD. It would.

KASSIE. What's going to happen?

CONRAD. Your son will start up with your brother's nurse. They've been waiting for each other. There, for the taking. And they'll take it.

KASSIE. Good luck to them. Jesus, it starts again. The rigmarole of life. The pain.

CONRAD. It always does. And we can do nothing to change it.

KASSIE. Nothing.

CONRAD. Is it worth the effort? Is it, Kassie?

KASSIE. Yes, Conrad. I believe it is.

(GABRIEL screams in the bedroom.)

Scene Seven

(ALMA holds GABRIEL's hand as he lies in bed. The screen dividing the living room and bedroom has disappeared.)

GABRIEL. The whispers come, the whispers go,
    They each echo over the sea,
    A foreign land and a foreign strand
    Have taken you from me.
    Oh do you remember – remember –

    (silence)

    How do you spell remember?

    (ALMA spells the word for him.)

    My mother was an excellent speller. She used to read dictionaries.

ALMA. I'm getting better at it.

GABRIEL. Yes.

    (ALMA's hand goes to GABRIEL's face. He takes her hand and bites it.)

ALMA. You bit me.

GABRIEL. Did I draw blood?

    (ALMA bites GABRIEL's hand.)

    My tiny hand is poisoned.

ALMA. So is mine.

GABRIEL. Why do you think I bit it?

    (silence)

    Will Ryan come back?

ALMA. No. He's on his own.

GABRIEL. Do you want him to?

ALMA. What do you think?

GABRIEL. Good.

    (They laugh lowly.)

    What is the night like?

ALMA. Clean. The beginnings of a new moon.

GABRIEL. Waxing and waning.

ALMA. The moon is really beautiful tonight. Do you know one of the first things I remember? We were on holiday in Kerry, and my father woke me up to watch the moon landing. It was the middle of the night and Valentia Island where we were staying was quiet. It's always quiet there, you can only hear the sea. We sat there, listening to the water, looking at human beings walking on another world, in the dark night.

GABRIEL. I love that memory.

ALMA. You can have it.

(silence)

You want to see Conrad?

GABRIEL. Yes, I do.

ALMA. I'll get him.

GABRIEL. Do.

ALMA. Goodnight.

GABRIEL. Goodbye.

(She goes to **CONRAD.** *She nods.)*

CONRAD. You'll not leave us.

ALMA. No. I'll stay here.

(She watches him go to the bedside. She goes behind the armchair. She touches it. She sits down on it.)

GABRIEL. O Jesus, It's Medea.

*(**CONRAD** sits.)*

Come to kill your children, darling? You're a little late. They passed away some time ago. They were never born. All those useless nights in this useless bed when we entertained our fantasies, but there is nothing left. It was all for nothing. All you have is me. And am I worth having? Do I break your hardened heart? I do hope so. That's what you deserved. What you wanted. Fuck you. You've got it.

CONRAD. Well, you're in flying form tonight.

GABRIEL. Not really, no.

CONRAD. Oh boo-hoo, poor you.

GABRIEL. Are you coming to bed?

CONRAD. Not yet.

GABRIEL. Are you going to sit there all night?

CONRAD. If I have to.

GABRIEL. Until I say I'm sorry, is that it? I want you to come to bed. Your bed, our bed. Happy bed, where I have loved you for a long time and lived with you for an eternity. For that, I am sorry. Now get into the fucking bed. It's late.

(CONRAD *sits beside* GABRIEL *and takes him in his arms.*)

Tell me a goodnight story. Give me a fantasy.

CONRAD. What kind?

GABRIEL. Us.

CONRAD. Two men met. They had a marriage. It lasted. Then one man was dying, and the other let him. He held this good man, this great man in his arms, for though they hurt and could hate each other more than man could bear, he did not want to let the love of his life pass away. He said, 'Stay with me, obey me,' but love is not obedient, for it must defy all the odds and that is why it lasts. My most disobedient, my most defiant, my most strange boy, and we will outlast all the lies we've ever told each other. I have achieved nothing without you. How do I say, without you? For then there is nothing, I am nothing, but you tried to make me something. This something lets me tell you I believe you. I always have. Are you alive? Breathe.

(*silence*)

Gabriel, breathe.

GABRIEL. Open the door. Open the gate. The gates of gold.

(*They kiss.*)

Also by
Frank McGuinness...

Observe the Sons of Ulster
Marching Toward the Somme

Someone Who'll Watch Over Me

Also available from Samuel French

THE BOYS IN THE BAND
Mart Crowley

Drama / 9m/ Interior

This seminal work of the Off-Broadway movement premiered in 1968 and was a long-running hit onstage, later filmed with the original cast. In 2010, the play made a triumphant return to New York City in an highly praised production produced by Drama Desk and Obie Award winning Transport Group.

In his upper eastside Manhattan apartment, Michael is throwing a birthday party for Harold, a self-avowed "32 year-old, pock-marked, Jew fairy", complete with surprise gift: "Cowboy," a street hustler. As the evening wears on, fueled by drugs and alcohol, bitter, unresolved resentments among the guests come to light when a game of "Truth" goes terribly wrong.

"A play of real substance, one that deserves to be performed not occasionally but regularly."
– The Wall Street Journal

"...terrifically thoughtful...The Boys in the Band emerges remarkably universal."
- NY1

"...deliriously delicious..."
– Gay City News

"The Boys in the Band... goes from wittily bitchy to heart-breakingly brutal..."
– Out Magazine

Please visit our website **samuelfrench.com** for complete descriptions and licensing information

LaVergne, TN USA
02 September 2010
195503LV00007B/6/P